POKÉMON®
DELUXE ACTIVITY BOOK
JOHTO EDITION

60 PAGES OF PUZZLES AND GAMES!

How well do you know the Johto Pokémon? There are some very unusual legends about this fascinating bunch. And this book is full of Johto Pokémon puzzles! You'll even find some trivia and activities you can share with your friends. All you need is a pencil, and you're ready to go. Let's get started!

ISBN 978-0-545-17721-4

12 11 10 9 8 7 6 5 4 3 2 1   10 11 12 13 14 15/0

Written by Katherine Fang
Interior Design by Kay Petronio   Cover Design by Henry Ng
Printed in the U.S.A.   40
First printing, April 2010

SCHOLASTIC INC.
New York   Toronto   London   Auckland
Sydney   Mexico City   New Delhi   Hong Kong

TRUE OR FALSE?

LUGIA

HEIGHT: 17' 01"
WEIGHT: 476.2 LBS

TYPE: PSYCHIC / FLYING

HO-OH

HEIGHT: 12' 06"
WEIGHT: 438.7 LBS

TYPE: FIRE / FLYING

CELEBI

HEIGHT: 2' 00"
WEIGHT: 11 LBS

TYPE: PSYCHIC / GRASS

Lugia, Ho-Oh, and Celebi are three of Johto's Legendary Pokémon. There are many fascinating stories about these Pokémon. Do you know which of the tales below are true and which are false?

○ TRUE ○ FALSE 1. Lugia is famous for the power of its roar.

○ TRUE ○ FALSE 2. Lugia can calm even a raging storm.

○ TRUE ○ FALSE 3. Lugia lives high in the mountains.

○ TRUE ○ FALSE 4. Lugia is known as the Diving Pokémon.

○ TRUE ○ FALSE 5. Lugia's Aeroblast move can also be learned by Ho-Oh.

○ TRUE ○ FALSE 6. Ho-Oh has the power to make people wealthy.

○ TRUE ○ FALSE 7. Ho-Oh's wings can shine in seven colors.

○ TRUE ○ FALSE 8. Ho-Oh's special Ability is Intimidate.

○ TRUE ○ FALSE 9. Ho-Oh lives at the base of a mountain.

○ TRUE ○ FALSE 10. Ho-Oh is the only Pokémon that knows the Sacred Fire move.

○ TRUE ○ FALSE 11. Celebi only appears in times of trouble.

○ TRUE ○ FALSE 12. Celebi has the power to travel through time.

○ TRUE ○ FALSE 13. Celebi is called the guardian of the forest.

○ TRUE ○ FALSE 14. Celebi's special Ability is Serene Grace.

○ TRUE ○ FALSE 15. Celebi can cause plants to grow wherever it goes.

TRIVIA TIME!

1 Which Pokémon flies over 180 miles per hour?

A. Ledyba   C. Noctowl

B. Skarmory   D. Misdreavus

2 Which Pokémon is less than two feet tall, but strong enough to carry a person on its back?

A. Skiploom   C. Swinub

B. Togepi   D. Phanpy

3 Which Pokémon is also called the "Deep-Sea Star"?

A. Mantine   C. Lanturn

B. Qwilfish   D. Remoraid

4 Which Pokémon hops around spiny plants looking for food?

A. Natu   C. Hoothoot

B. Delibird   D. Murkrow

5 When these Pokémon gather in groups, they can form a platform strong enough to support a house!

A. Pineco   C. Corsola

B. Shuckle   D. Pupitar

6 When this Pokémon uses psychic power, a jewel on its forehead will glow.

A. Espeon   C. Sneasel

B. Slowking   D. Ampharos

DELIBIRD'S DELIVERY!

Delibird wants to deliver presents. But it forgot which Pokémon should get the gifts! Can you help Delibird? Fill in the blanks by combining the word fragments below to make Pokémon names.

swinub

SWI

CHU

TURN

KERN

BULL

SNUB

CHOU

LAN

SUN

PI

NUB

CHIN

SMEARGLE'S CONNECT-THE DOTS

Smeargle can use its tail lik... ...trying to paint? Connect the dots to ...ture!

Smeargle can use its tail to make over 5,000 different marks!

TRUE TO TYPE!

Every Pokémon belongs to at least one type. Each of the Pokémon here has just one type—can you match them?

Dunsparce	Bug
Slugma	Dark
Sunflora	Electric
Azumarill	Fighting
Sudowoodo	Fire
Mareep	Ghost
Tyrogue	Grass
Pineco	Normal
Misdreavus	Rock
Umbreon	Water

MAKING A SPLASH!

Dive into this word search to find Pokémon who live in Johto's rivers, lakes, and seas! To see them all, you'll have to look up, down, forward, backward, and even diagonally!

```
B  E  R  I  S  G  A  U  Q  E  S  R
A  K  C  Y  U  T  S  W  H  Z  M  E
Z  M  O  H  E  N  I  T  N  A  M  M
U  E  N  F  I  L  M  G  R  C  L  O
M  S  L  E  F  N  I  E  A  F  Y  R
A  B  L  I  P  E  C  L  N  O  S  A
R  O  S  G  D  K  H  H  B  E  T  I
I  H  U  L  C  O  R  S  O  L  A  D
L  Y  E  N  A  U  T  L  D  U  M  B
L  D  S  Z  W  F  S  O  E  N  J  R
I  L  A  N  T  U  R  N  T  Z  T  O
E  G  Y  R  E  L  L  I  T  C  O  N
```

Azumarill
Chinchou
Corsola

Lanturn
Mantine
Octillery
Quagsire

Qwilfish
Remoraid
Totodile

HOPPIP AND AWAY!

Hoppip are so small and light, they can float on the breeze! A strong wind scattered these Hoppip all over the field. Can you help them find one another? Locate the path through the maze that connects all the lost Hoppip!

start

finish

EVOLUTION TUTOR

These Pokémon can't evolve until they learn a special move. Can you help them evolve? Match each Pokémon to the move it needs to evolve!

HINT: Not all of these moves will be used. Some moves may be used more than once!

Aipom + _____ → **Ambipom**

Yanma + _____ → **Yanmega**

Bonsly + _____ → **Sudowoodo**

Piloswine + _____ → **Mamoswine**

AncientPower   Double Hit
DoubleSlap   Hidden Power
Substitute   Mimic

NAME SCRAMBLE

Slowking is as smart as a scientist, but don't let it stump you! Unscramble the Pokémon names. Then write down the highlighted letters from each name to reveal one of Slowking's secrets.

1. YOTEGUR ___ ___ ___ ___ ___ ___ ___

2. WCOANCOR ___ ___ ___ ___ ___ ___ ___ ___

3. NRRAITATY ___ ___ ___ ___ ___ ___ ___ ___ ___

4. KTMAILN ___ ___ ___ ___ ___ ___ ___

5. VSEDMURASI ___ ___ ___ ___ ___ ___ ___ ___ ___ ___

6. GGOAMCRA ___ ___ ___ ___ ___ ___ ___ ___

7. HOTMPOINT ___ ___ ___ ___ ___ ___ ___ ___ ___

8. HCNUHCIO ___ ___ ___ ___ ___ ___ ___ ___

If Slowking has this Ability, it can't be Confused. That's because it follows its

◯◯◯ ◯◯◯◯◯◯ !
___ ___ ___ ___ ___ ___ ___ ___ ___

WHAT'S IN A NAME?

Can you match each Pokémon with the name of its species?

Long Tail Pokémon	Aipom
Water Fish Pokémon	Ariados
Screech Pokémon	Chinchou
Dragon Pokémon	Girafarig
Hard Shell Pokémon	Kingdra
Long Leg Pokémon	Ledian
Five Star Pokémon	Misdreavus
Long Neck Pokémon	Pupitar
Royal Pokémon	Slowking
Angler Pokémon	Wooper

ALL SQUARE

Fill in each box so that Chikorita, Cyndaquil, Totodile, and Pichu appear only once in each horizontal, vertical, or diagonal row of 4. Each Pokémon only appears once in each 2x2 box, too!

Cyndaquil

Totodile

Chikorita

Pichu

SOUND THE HORN!

Some Johto Pokémon have unique horns. Look at the close-ups below and identify their owner!

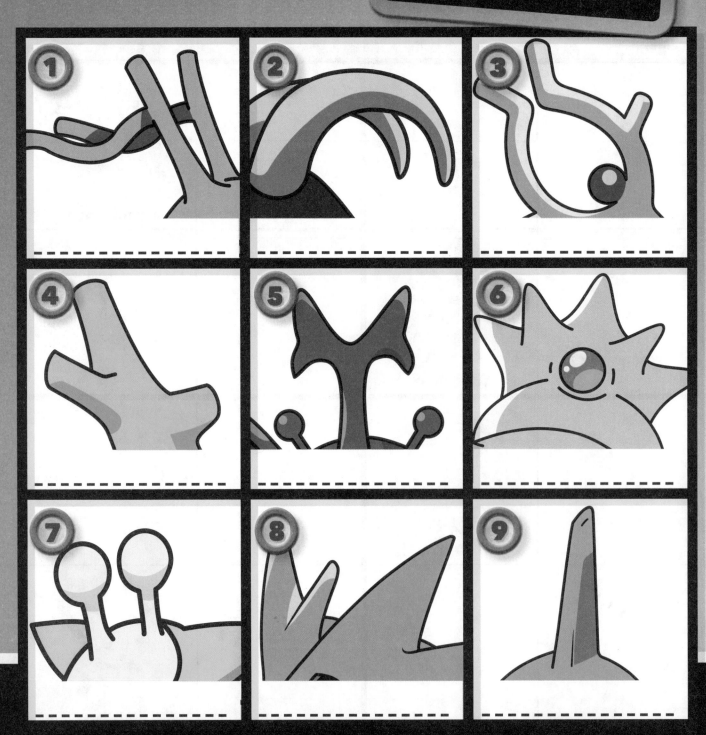

CROSSWORD

ACROSS

1. Jigglypuff's pre-evolved form
7. The Spike Ball Pokémon
8. Not Entei or Suicune, but _____
9. This Pokémon's only move is Sketch.
11. In the Pokédex, it is after Kingdra but before Donphan.
12. The evolved form of Golbat
13. A blue and white Legendary Pokémon

DOWN

2. A basic Normal-type move that lowers Attack
3. A basic Normal-type move that lowers Defense
4. This Pokémon can sense sad feelings.
5. It evolves from Sentret.
6. Donphan and Miltank can both learn this spinning attack.
10. Xatu's pre-evolved form

MISSING LINKS

The vowels are missing from the Pokémon names below. Do you know which Pokémon is which?

1. CRBT _____
2. SNSL _____
3. BYLF _____
4. SPN _____
5. LKD _____
6. PNC _____
7. MRP _____
8. PCH _____
9. LDN _____
10. QLV _____
11. TGP _____
12. RDS _____

ALL TOGETHER NOW

Each set of Pokémon has something in common. Can you figure out what it is?

A	B	C	D	E
Mantine	Hitmontop	Togepi	Tyranitar	Bellossom
Skarmory	Stantler	Smeargle	Steelix	Crobat
Gligar	Snubbull	Ursaring	Dunsparce	Houndoom

1. All of these Pokémon are Normal-types. _____

2. All of these Pokémon can have the Intimidate Ability. _____

3. All of these Pokémon can be found in rocky places. _____

4. All of these Pokémon are final evolved forms. _____

5. All of these Pokémon are Flying-types. _____

WHERE ARE THE WOOPER?

Fun Fact:
When it walks on dry land, Water-type Wooper coats its body with a slimy, poisonous film.

FOLLOW THE LEGEND

Trainers search long and hard to find Johto's Legendary Pokémon. But you can find Legendary Pokémon right here! Solve the problem under each space. Then look up the answer in the key. Fill in the letter that belongs in each space, and crack the Legendary code!

This Pokémon runs on the wind and purifies water.

___	___	___	___	___	___	___
10-3	12 / 2	3+5	8-3	2x3	5+5	3+6

This Legendary Pokémon carries rain clouds on its back.

___	___	___	___	___	___
12 / 3	7-4	4x2	6-4	3x4	9-3

This Legendary Pokémon has a roar that makes volcanoes erupt.

___	___	___	___	___
4+5	2x5	6-5	3x3	9-1

A: 3   I: 8   O: 12   T: 1
C: 5   K: 2   R: 4   U: 6
E: 9   N: 10   S: 7

WHAT TYPE?

Even Legendary Pokémon have their strengths and weaknesses. How much do you know about Raikou, Entei, and Suicune?

RAIKOU
Type: Electric
Height: 6' 03"
Weight: 392.4 lbs

ENTEI
Type: Fire
Height: 6' 11"
Weight: 436.5 lbs

SUICUNE
Type: Water
Height: 6' 07"
Weight: 412.3 lbs

 1. Which of these types is Raikou strong against?
Flying   Rock   Steel   Poison

 2. Which of these types is super-effective against Raikou?
Ground   Grass   Fire   Rock

 3. Which of these types is Entei strong against?
Psychic   Fighting   Flying   Bug

 4. Which of these types is super-effective against Entei?
Electric   Water   Rock   Ground

 5. Which of these types is Suicune strong against?
Water   Ice   Steel   Poison

 6. Which of these types is super-effective against Suicune?
Grass   Dragon   Dark   Electric

DINNER TIME!

Professor Elm is looking after the Pokémon at his lab. That means feeding them, too! Help Professor Elm make these eight Pokémon happy. Circle the food that's best for each Pokémon!

1 What food does Teddiursa like?

Twigs   Honey   Eggs

2 What does Larvitar consume for energy?

Soil   Grass   Sunlight

3 What does Swinub like to eat?

Ice   Moss   Mushrooms

4 What does Heracross like to eat?

Tree Sap   Berries   Vegetables

5 Where does Ledian get its energy?

Sunlight   Starlight   Moonlight

6 What does Marill like to eat?

Aquatic Plants   Roots   Tree Bark

7 What does Aipom like to eat?

Seeds   Fruit   Leaves

8 What does Sneasel like to eat?

Rocks   Eggs   Nuts

SHADOW TAG

Can you tell these Johto Pokémon apart by their shadows?

 **1** _____

 **2**

Espeon

 **3** _____

 **4**

Feraligatr

Typhlosion

Umbreon

 **5** _____

 **6**

Quagsire

Wobbuffet

FOLLOWING YOUR FOOTSTEPS

A new trainer wants to tell her friends about some of the places she's visited in Johto. But she's forgotten the order in which she visited each city! Help her figure out the order of the four places she visited.

CLUE 1: "Blackthorn City was the last place I visited."

_____

CLUE 2: "I went to Violet City before I went to Ecruteak City."

_____

CLUE 3: "Goldenrod City was not the first place I visited."

_____

CLUE 4: "I went to Ecruteak City after I went to Goldenrod City."

_____

Can you figure out the order of the trainer's trip?

THE NAME OF THE GAME

What do the stories say about Ho-Oh? Use the first letter of each Pokémon's name to find out!

Legends say that Ho-Oh lives at the foot of a

__ __ __ __ __ __ __ .

But legends also say that Ho-Oh may appear at Johto's

__ __ __

__ __ __ __ __ !

NOCTOWL'S NIGHT VISION!

Noctowl has great eyesight. It can see even in dim light! What Pokémon does Noctowl see? Connect the dots to find out!

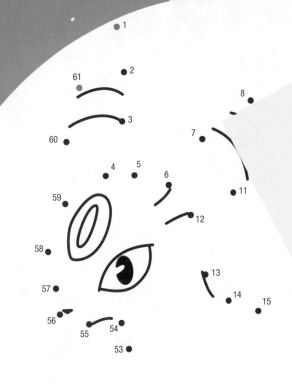

1
61 2
8
3
60 7
4 5 6 11
59 12
58 13
57 14 15
56 55 54 53

52 25
42 26
43 35
51 41 34 27
44 36 33
50 45 40 32
49 39 38 37 31 28
46 30 29
47
48

if Noctowl flips its head over, that doesn't mean it can't see. It means Noctowl is thinking!

CROSSWORD

ACROSS

3. The Kiss Pokémon
7. The Legendary Guardian of the Seas
8. The Psychic-type Evolution of Eevee
9. A rare Pokémon type that is weak against ice-types
10. The Pokémon that can see the past and future
11. The final evolved form of Horsea

DOWN

1. The Water Fish Pokémon
2. The evolved form of Ledyba
3. At 30' 02" long, it is the longest Pokémon in Johto.
4. Its name rhymes with "hour."
5. A Pokémon with nutritious milk
6. A Pokémon that evolves from Totodile

HIP TO BE SQUARE

Fill in each box so that Raikou, Entei, Suicune, and Pichu appear only once in each horizontal, vertical, or diagonal row of 4. Each Pokémon only appears once in each 2x2 box, too!

Entei

Suicune

Raikou

Pichu

A TANGLED WEB

START

FINISH

TRIVIA TIME 2

1 Which Pokémon scatters spores as it travels around the world?

A. Delibird   B. Ledian

C. Jumpluff   D. Shuckle

2 Which Pokémon can give off a spicy aroma to energize people?

A. Sunflora   B. Bayleef

C. Bellossom   D. Skiploom

3 Which Pokémon can use a jet of gas to rocket into the air?

A. Pupitar   B. Mantine

C. Kingdra   D. Octillery

4 Misdreavus feeds off fear that it absorbs with its:

A. Yellow eyes   B. Loud cry

C. Purple shadow   D. Red orbs

5 The patterns on Scizor's _____ are used to intimidate foes.

A. Wings   B. Legs

C. Pincers   D. Back

6 Which Pokémon is capable of operating in space?

A. Skarmory   B. Porygon2

C. Ho-Oh   D. Lugia

TEST YOUR MEMORY!

Xatu stares at the sun all day. (Don't try that at home!) But you just have to stare at the box below for thirty seconds. Then turn the page and see how many questions you can answer!

This game is fun to play with friends, too!

CHECK YOUR MEMORY!

Do you remember what you saw on page 31? Don't worry if you can't answer every question. This is a tough challenge!

1 How many Ledyba were there? _____

2 How many Ledian were there? _____

3 How many Slugma were there? _____

4 How many Pokémon were on the page? _____

5 How many different kinds of Pokémon were there? _____

6 What kinds of Pokémon were on the page? _____

ALL IN ORDER

The Evolutions below are all mixed up. Fill in the correct Evolution order!

1 Chansey → Happiny → Blissey

_____ → _____ → _____

2 Swinub → Mamoswine → Piloswine

_____ → _____ → _____

3 Gloom → Oddish → Bellossom

_____ → _____ → _____

4 Poliwhirl → Poliwag → Politoed

_____ → _____ → _____

5 Togekiss → Togetic → Togepi

_____ → _____ → _____

6 Skiploom → Hoppip → Jumpluff

_____ → _____ → _____

GRIDLOCKED!

There are twelve Pokémon words hidden in this grid. Put your pencil on the letter E and move up, down, left, or right to form a word. Can you use all the letters once without lifting your pencil?

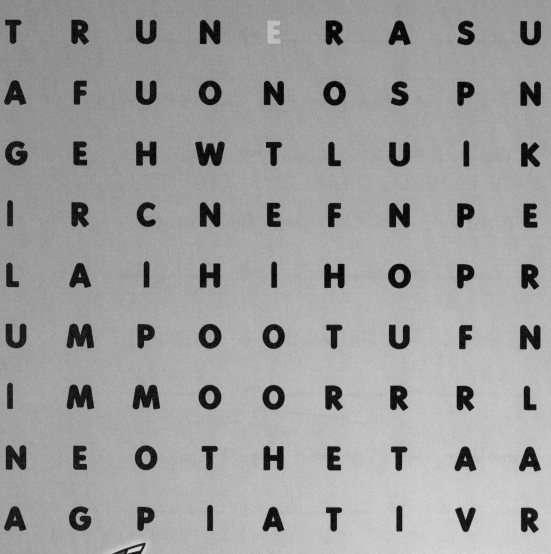

```
T   R   U   N   E   R   A   S   U
A   F   U   O   N   O   S   P   N
G   E   H   W   T   L   U   I   K
I   R   C   N   E   F   N   P   E
L   A   I   H   I   H   O   P   R
U   M   P   O   O   T   U   F   N
I   M   M   O   O   R   R   R   L
N   E   O   T   H   E   T   A   A
A   G   P   I   A   T   I   V   R
```

A PICTURE PUZZLER

Igglybuff: _____, _____, _____

Cleffa: _____, _____, _____

Blissey: _____, _____, _____

THREE'S A CROWD

In Johto, Professor Elm gives new trainers their first Pokémon. Three trainers have come to Professor Elm today. Read what each trainer says about the Pokémon they want. Then help Professor Elm pick the right Pokémon for each trainer!

CHIKORITA

Type: Grass
Height: 2' 11"
Weight: 14.1 lbs.

CYNDAQUIL

Type: Fire
Height: 1' 08"
Weight: 17.4 lbs.

TOTODILE

Type: Water
Height: 2' 00"
Weight: 20.9 lbs.

Trainer A:

I like Fire-type and Water-type Pokémon.
The smaller the Pokémon, the more I like it!

The best Pokémon for Trainer A is _____.

Trainer B:

I don't like Fire-type Pokémon.
I want a Pokémon that is more than two feet tall.

The best Pokémon for Trainer B is _____.

Trainer C:

I like Water-type and Grass-type Pokémon.
I want a Pokémon that weighs more than fifteen pounds.

The best Pokémon for Trainer C is _____.

ALL THE RIGHT MOVES!

What set of moves goes with each Pokémon?

1. Miltank _____
2. Sneasel _____
3. Forretress _____
4. Furret _____
5. Shuckle _____
6. Porygon2 _____
7. Qwilfish _____
8. Girafarig _____

A.	**B.**	**C.**	**D.**
Stomp	Quick Attack	Recycle	Heal Bell
Psychic	Me First	Conversion	Rollout
Power Swap	Hyper Voice	Lock-On	Stomp
Double Hit	Baton Pass	Discharge	Milk Drink

E.	**F.**	**G.**	**H.**
Poison Sting	Ice Shard	Withdraw	Iron Defense
Pin Missile	Fury Swipes	Gastro Acid	Zap Cannon
Aqua Tail	Slash	Wrap	Rapid Spin
Toxic Spikes	Metal Claw	Bide	Selfdestruct

HEADS OR TAILS?

Ampharos
Dunsparce
Girafarig
Gligar

Marill
Sentret
Wobbuffet

1 This Pokémon's tail can glow in the dark. _____

2 This Pokémon's tail can float. _____

3 This Pokémon's tail is said to hide a secret. _____

4 This Pokémon balances on its tail so it can sit up and look around. _____

5 This Pokémon's tail has a poison stinger. _____

6 This Pokémon uses its tail to dig itself a nest. _____

7 This Pokémon's tail may have a brain of its own. _____

NAME-CALLING

Some Pokémon have the same species names. Match the Pokémon to the right species!

1 Which Pokémon are known as Sun Pokémon?

_____ and _____

2 Which Pokémon are known as Light Pokémon?

_____ and _____

3 Which Pokémon are known as Armor Pokémon?

_____ and _____

4 Which Pokémon are known as Volcano Pokémon?

_____ and _____

5 Which Pokémon are known as Happiness Pokémon?

_____ and _____

6 Which Pokémon are known as Balloon Pokémon?

_____ and _____

Ampharos	Espeon	Qwilfish
Blissey	Igglybuff	Sunflora
Donphan	Lanturn	Togetic
Entei	Quilava	Tyranitar

39

MORE MISSING LINKS!

The vowels are missing from the Pokémon names below. Do you know which Pokémon is which?

1. NT _____

2. RK _____

3. SCN _____

4. CLB _____

5. H-H _____

6. LG _____

7. PM _____

8. NWN _____

9. XT _____

10. HTHT _____

THE KEY TO EVOLUTION

Some Pokémon can use an item to evolve. Can you help these Pokémon? Match the right item to the right Pokémon. Then write in the Pokémon's evolved form!

HINT:
Not every item will be used. Some items may be used more than once!

1 **Gligar** + _____ → _____

2 **Murkrow** + _____ → _____

3 **Sunkern** + _____ → _____

4 **Togetic** + _____ → _____

5 **Sneasel** + _____ → _____

6 **Misdreavus** + _____ → _____

Dusk Stone	Oval Stone	Sun Stone
King's Rock	Razor Claw	Shiny Stone
Metal Coat	Razor Fang	

TWO HEADS ARE BETTER THAN ONE

Some Johto Pokémon have connections to other Pokémon. Can you figure out which Pokémon belong in these sentences? We'll even get you started with the first letter of each Pokémon's name.

1 R_____ latches on to M _____ to feed on its leftover scraps.

2 Why is S_____ so smart? Somehow, it's because it was bitten by S_____ .

3 P_____ can use its cries to make P_____ obey.

NIGHT SHIFT!

Ash and Pikachu are lost in the forest. That could be dangerous — it's late at night and the forest is full of wild Pokémon! Can you help Ash and Pikachu? See if you can spot them . . . and all the other Pokémon!

```
U  M  U  R  K  R  O  W  O  A  I  Y  L
D  E  N  L  E  N  T  E  R  S  B  W  C
K  M  U  H  C  A  K  I  P  V  O  M  K
N  S  M  K  U  W  A  V  U  T  N  R  E
O  T  B  E  R  D  J  R  C  H  A  S  H
C  I  R  V  O  S  E  O  E  G  R  B  S
N  R  E  S  U  C  N  T  S  U  O  P  L
B  H  O  L  W  Y  C  K  W  D  I  C  A
P  V  N  B  I  R  U  O  D  N  U  O  H
A  Y  N  R  A  N  I  H  A  B  C  S  I
U  N  E  S  O  T  M  R  T  P  K  W  P
M  I  S  D  R  E  A  V  U  S  E  I  N
E  K  R  J  A  K  V  D  N  O  K  U  R
```

Ariados	Misdreavus	Spinarak
Ash	Murkrow	Umbreon
Crobat	Noctowl	
Houndour	Pikachu	

A DIZZY DILEMMA

Hitmontop spins on its head to power up its moves. But this Hitmontop spun until it got dizzy! Now it has its attack names all mixed up. Can you help Hitmontop? Correct these mixed-up moves!

_____ _____

_____ _____

_____ _____

_____ _____

_____ _____

_____ _____

_____ _____

_____ _____

Rapid Kick **Close Attack** **Brick Power**

Rolling Energy **Hidden Break** **Quick Spin**

Gyro Combat **Focus Ball**

PLACING AN ORDER

Number these Pokémon from the heaviest (1) to the lightest (4)!

Donphan _____

Azumarill _____

Tyranitar _____

Heracross _____

Number these Pokémon from the shortest (1) to the tallest (4)!

Scizor _____

Sunflora _____

Igglybuff _____

Quagsire _____

Who's heavier, Smeargle or Skarmory? The answer will surprise you! Smeargle weighs 127.9 pounds, but Skarmory only weighs 111.3 pounds.

NO PLACE LIKE HOME!

Where are you most likely to find each Pokémon? Draw a line from each Pokémon to the place where it lives!

Bellossom

Crobat

Girafarig

Heracross

cave

forest

grassland

Hoppip

Misdreavus

Pineco

Wobbuffet

Noctowl

LEARN TO TYPE!

Each of these Pokémon has two types, not one!
Can you match the right types to each Pokémon?

1 HERACROSS   _____   _____

2 HOUNDOOM   _____   _____

3 GIRAFARIG   _____   _____

4 SKARMORY   _____   _____

5 KINGDRA   _____   _____

6 PILOSWINE   _____   _____

Dark	Fire	Ground
Flying	Normal	Psychic
Fighting	Bug	Water
Dragon	Steel	Ice

UNOWN CODE

There are twenty-six different forms of Unown on these pages. Each one looks like a letter of the alphabet. But the Unown are all out of order! Can you still tell what letter or mark each Unown represents?

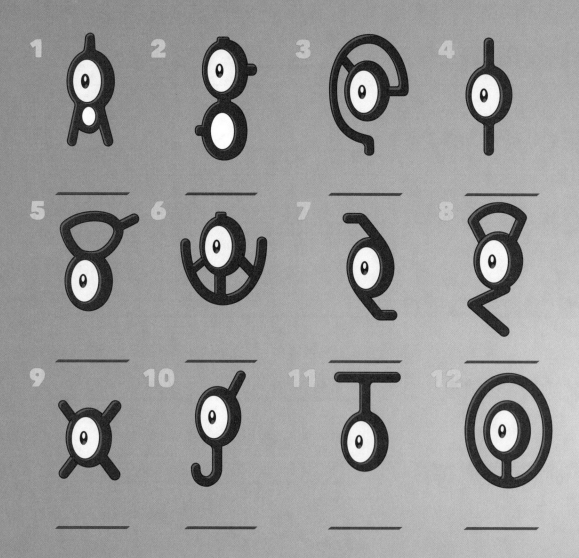

1. _____
2. _____
3. _____
4. _____
5. _____
6. _____
7. _____
8. _____
9. _____
10. _____
11. _____
12. _____

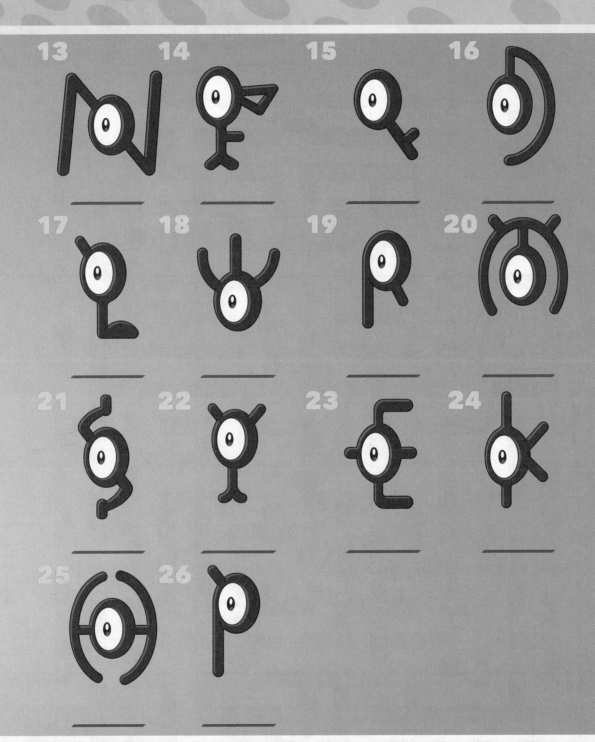

NERVES OF STEELIX!

Steelix can burrow through tunnels in the ground. Sometimes Rock-type Pokémon live in those tunnels, ~~intruders! Can~~ ~~Steelix's tunnels~~ ~~any Pokémon?~~

START ▶▶

FINISH

GR **KED!**

There are twelve [...] [...]d. Put your pencil on the letter M and [...] [...]rm a word. Can you use all the letters [...]

```
T U [    ] [ ] A T Y
A C H O R U G O R
N U I A R E T L E
A T K P I S N O R
X U O E M T A C T
S T O G A N O I I
O D K E G P H S L
I A I L B Y L O L
R A D E Y T Y R E
```

MAKING A MARK!

Some Johto Pokémon have very unusual markings. Can you match each marking to the Pokémon it belongs to?

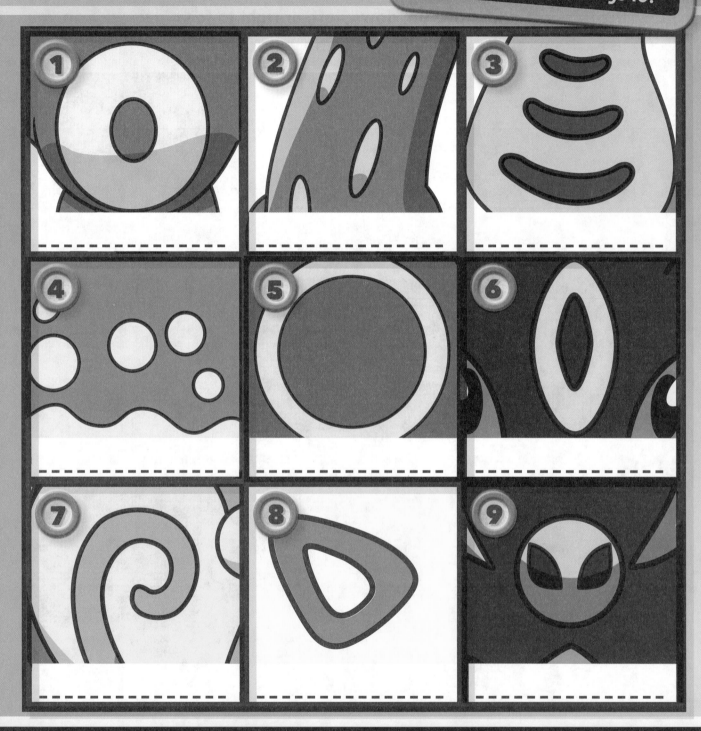

Azumarill
Politoed
Sentret

Sudowoodo
Togepi
Umbreon

Ursaring
Wooper
Houndoom

CRYPTIC CLUES

Each of the numbers below stands for a letter. Can you break the code? We'll give you a hint: 1=A and 5=E!

1 This Pokémon is more numerous in the year after a cold summer.

——— ——— ——— ——— ——— ——— ———
19   21   14   11   5   18   14

2 This Pokémon looks fierce, but is much more timid than it seems.

——— ——— ——— ——— ——— ——— ——— ———
7   18   1   14   2   21   12   12

3 Some Pokémon have keen eyes or good noses. This Pokémon has sensitive lips!

——— ——— ——— ——— ——— ——— ——— ———
19   13   15   15   3   8   21   13

4 This Pokémon sometimes hits its head on rocks as it moves, but does not care.

——— ——— ——— ——— ——— ——— ——— ———
17   21   1   7   19   9   18   5

EVOLUTION CHALLENGE

Fill in each Evolution chain with the Pokémon that belong in the blanks!

1 _____ → **Flaaffy** → _____

2 **Cyndaquil** → _____ → _____

3 _____ → **Pupitar** → _____

4 _____ → _____ → **Kingdra**

5 _____ → _____ → **Azumarill**

6 **Cleffa** → _____ → _____

Tyrogue can evolve into three different Pokémon! Can you name them all?

7 **Tyrogue** → _____
_____
_____

FAIR AND SQUARE

Fill in each box so that Cleffa, Togepi, Magby, and Elekid appear only once in each horizontal, vertical, or diagonal row of 4. Each Pokémon only appears once in each 2x2 box, too!

Togepi

Magby

Cleffa

Elekid

WHO WAS IT?

Ash thought he saw a wild Pokémon, but it ran away before he had a good look. Can you help him figure out what Pokémon it was?

SCIZOR
Height: 5' 11"
Weight: 260.1 lbs.

WOBBUFFET
Height: 4' 03"
Weight: 62.8 lbs.

PILOSWINE
Height: 3' 07"
Weight: 123.0 lbs.

GIRAFARIG
Height: 4' 11"
Weight: 91.5 lbs.

CLUE 1: The Pokémon was at least 4' 00" tall.

CLUE 2: The Pokémon looked like it had four eyes.

CLUE 3: The Pokémon had a tail.

CLUE 4: The Pokémon looked like it weighed more than eighty pounds.

Which Pokémon was it? _____

GOOD THINGS COME IN SMALL PACKAGES

...earch may be ...full of small ...Can you find

Out of all the Pokémon in this puzzle, Natu is the smallest. It's only eight inches tall!

L P O E N S N ... ... O
J I B U N I W S X E D Q U B
M P R W A T G B R L U T A N
U P S O T N E A Y E R M L I
E O R O K E T O A K E W B P
T H Q P J I D B N I O R I H
C A B E V U S D R D X C H A
J R I R Y A N J I R H G O N
C S A E M T R K E U E Y M P
P L M T O G E P I Z R A U Y
E U E C R M K R H E G S D F
L N Z F I A N E F B O N A T
K O R U F F U B Y L G G I O
L E D Y B A S J E T D E B W

Cleffa	Larvitar	Phanpy	Swinub
Elekid	Ledyba	Pichu	Teddiursa
Hoppip	Magby	Snubbull	Togepi
Igglybuff	Natu	Sunkern	Wooper

TRIVIA TIME 3

Are you ready for your final set of trivia questions? Then let's go!

1 Which Pokémon can spin its arms to generate electricity?

A. Flaaffy   B. Elekid

C. Ampharos   D. Pichu

2 Which Pokémon always keeps moving so its magma body doesn't cool down?

A. Magby   B. Houndoom

C. Slugma   D. Typhlosion

3 When this Pokémon bites, it won't let go until its fangs fall out! (Don't worry; its fangs will grow back!)

A. Houndour   B. Granbull

C. Croconaw   D. Tyranitar

4 Qwilfish is a prickly-looking Pokémon that can have the Poison Point Ability. What is the other Ability Qwilfish can have?

A. Hustle   B. Swift Swim

C. Water Absorb   D. Damp

5 In Johto, they say that when Togetic meets kind people, it will scatter a special down called:

A. Joy Dust   B. Aurora Dust

C. Poké Dust   D. Heart Dust

6 Which Pokémon has eyes that can see in all directions even behind it?

A. Xatu   B. Ledyba

C. Ariados   D. Yanma

TEST YOUR MEMORY 2!

Remember, no peeking! When you're done, turn the page to see how much you remember!

Here's a challenge for you to try! See if you can draw two Pokémon from memory in the spaces below. (You can ask your friends to try this, too!)

PIKACHU

WOBBUFFET

CHECK YOUR MEMORY 2!

Did you remember the spots on Pikachu's cheeks? Or Wobbuffet's tail? This was a tough challenge, so good work!

ANSWER KEY

Pages 2-3:
1. False, 2. True, 3. False, 4. True, 5. False, 6. False, 7. True, 8. False, 9. False, 10. True, 11. False, 12. True, 13. True, 14. False, 15. True

Page 4:
1. B
2. D
3. C
4. A
5. C
6. A

Page 5:
Chinchou, Lanturn, Pichu, Swinub, Snubbull, Sunkern

Page 6:

Page 7:
1. Normal, 2. Fire, 3. Grass, 4. Water, 5. Rock, 6. Electric, 7. Fighting, 8. Bug, 9. Ghost, 10. Dark

Page 8:

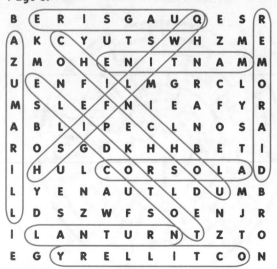

Page 9:

Page 10:
1. Double Hit, 2. AncientPower, 3. Mimic, 4. AncientPower

Page 11:
1. Tyrogue, 2. Croconaw, 3. Tyranitar, 4. Miltank, 5. Misdreavus, 6. Magcargo, 7. Hitmontop, 8. Chinchou; OWN TEMPO

Page 12:
1. Aipom, 2. Wooper, 3. Misdreavus, 4. Kingdra, 5. Pupitar, 6. Ariados, 7. Ledian, 8. Girafarig, 9. Slowking, 10. Chinchou

Page 13:

Page 14:
1. Kingdra, 2. Houndoom, 3. Stantler, 4. Corsola,
5. Heracross, 6. Slowking, 7. Girafarig, 8. Pupitar,
9. Levitar

Page 15:

Page 16:
1. Crobat, 2. Sneasel, 3. Bayleef, 4. Espeon, 5.
Elekid, 6. Pineco, 7. Mareep, 8. Pichu, 9. Ledian, 10.
Quilava, 11. Togepi, 12. Ariados

Page 17:
1. C, 2. B, 3. D, 4. E, 5. A

Pages 18-19:

Page 20:
1. Suicune, 2. Raikou, 3. Entei

Page 21:
1. Flying, Steel; 2. Ground; 3. Bug; 4. Water, Rock,
Ground; 5. Water, Ice, Steel; 6. Grass, Electric

Page 22:
1. Honey, 2. Soil, 3. Mushrooms, 4. Tree Sap, 5.
Starlight, 6. Aquatic Plants, 7. Fruit, 8. Eggs

Page 23:
1. Umbreon, 2. Espeon, 3. Quagsire, 4. Wobbuffet,
5. Feraligatr, 6. Typhlosion

Page 24:
The trainer went to Violet City, then Goldenrod
City, then Ecruteak City, then Blackthorn City.

Page 25:
Legends say that Ho-Oh lives at the foot of a
RAINBOW. But legends also say that Ho-Oh may
appear at Johto's TIN TOWER!

Page 26:

Page 27:

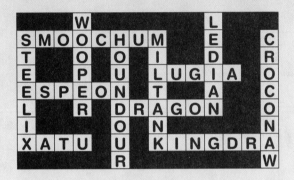

Page 28:

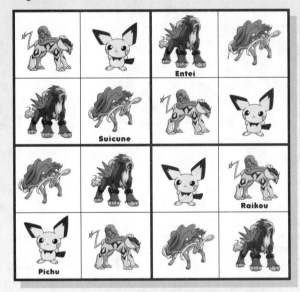

Page 29:

Page 30:
1. C, 2. B, 3. A, 4. D, 5. C, 6. B

Pages 31-32:
1. 3 Ledyba
2. 4 Ledian
3. 1 Slugma
4. 10
5. 5
6. Ledyba, Ledian, Slugma, Magcargo, Magby

Page 33:
1. Happiny, Chansey, Blissey
2. Swinub, Piloswine, Mamoswine
3. Oddish, Gloom, Bellossom
4. Poliwag, Poliwhirl, Politoed
5. Togepi, Togetic, Togekiss
6. Hoppip, Skiploom, Jumpluff

Page 34:

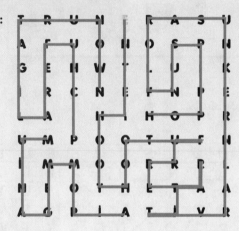

Page 35:
İgglybuff: 1, 6, 8
Cleffa: 3, 4, 7
Blissey: 2, 5, 9

Page 36:
Trainer A: Cyndaquil; Trainer B: Chikorita;
Trainer C: Totodile

Page 37:
1. D, 2. F, 3. H, 4. B, 5. G, 6. C, 7. E, 8. A

Page 38:
1. Ampharos
2. Marill
3. Wobbuffet
4. Sentret
5. Gligar
6. Dunsparce
7. Girafarig

Page 39:
1. Espeon, Sunflora; 2. Ampharos, Lanturn; 3. Donphan, Tyranitar; 4. Entei, Quilava; 5. Blissey, Togetic; 6. İgglybuff, Qwilfish

Page 40:
1. Entei or Natu, 2. Raikou, 3. Suicune, 4. Celebes, 5. Ho-Oh, 6. Lugia, 7. Aipom, 8. Unown, 9. Xatu, 10. Hoothoot

Page 41:
1. Razor Fang, Gliscor
2. Dusk Stone, Honchkrow
3. Sun Stone, Sunflora
4. Shiny Stone, Togekiss
5. Razor Claw, Weavile
6. Dusk Stone, Mismagius

Page 42:
1. Remoraid, Mantine
2. Slowking, Shellder
3. Politoed, Poliwag

Page 43:

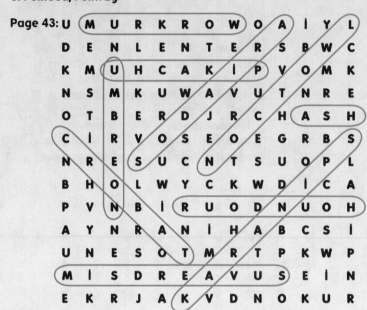

Page 44:
Rolling Kick
Focus Energy
Quick Attack
Rapid Spin
Gyro Ball
Close Combat
Brick Break
Hidden Power

Page 45:
Donphan   2
Azumarill   4
Tyranitar   1
Heracross   3

Scizor   4
Sunflora   2
İgglybuff   1
Quagsire   3

Page 46:
Cave: Crobat, Misdreavus, Wobbuffet
Forest: Heracross, Pineco, Noctowl
Grassland: Bellossom, Girafarig, Hoppip

Page 47:
1. Bug, Fighting; 2. Dark, Fire; 3. Normal, Psychic; 4. Steel, Flying; 5. Water, Dragon; 6. İce, Ground

Pages 48-49:
1. A, 2. B, 3. C, 4. İ, 5. V, 6. U, 7. Z, 8. G, 9. X, 10. J, 11. T, 12. O, 13. N, 14. F, 15. Q, 16. D, 17. L, 18. W, 19. R, 20. M, 21. S, 22. Y, 23. E, 24. K, 25. H, 26. P

Page 50:

Page 51:

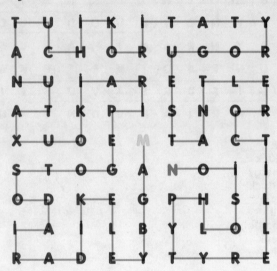

Page 52:
1. Sentret, 2. Sudowoodo, 3. Wooper, 4. Azumarill,
5. Ursaring, 6. Umbreon, 7. Politoed, 8. Togepi,
9. Houndoom

Page 53:
1. Sunkern, 2. Granbull, 3. Smoochum, 4. Quagsire

Page 54:

1. Mareep	Flaaffy	Ampharos
2. Cyndaquil	Quilava	Typhlosion
3. Larvitar	Pupitar	Tyranitar
4. Horsea	Seadra	Kingdra
5. Azurill	Marill	Azumarill
6. Cleffa	Clefairy	Clefable
7. Tyrogue	Hitmonlee, Hitmonchan, Hitmontop	

Page 55:

Page 56:
İt was a Girafarig.

Page 57:

Page 60:
1. B, 2. C, 3. C, 4. B, 5. A, 6. D